SILAS MARNER

SILAS MARNER

George Eliot

An imprint of Om Books International

First published in 2018 by

Om KIDZ | Om Books International

Corporate & Editorial Office
A-12, Sector 64, Noida 201 301
Uttar Pradesh, India
Phone: +91 120 477 4100
Email: editorial@ombooks.com
Website: www.ombooksinternational.com

Sales Office
107, Ansari Road, Darya Ganj
New Delhi 110 002, India
Phone: +91 11 4000 9000
Email: sales@ombooks.com
Website: www.ombooks.com

Retold by Swayam Ganguly

ISBN: 978-93-85031-64-9

Printed in India

10 9 8 7 6 5 4 3 2 1

Contents

Chapter One

A Gloomy Past

In the early nineteenth century, a linen-weaver called Silas Marner was busy at work in his stone cottage. This cottage stood with the nutty hedgerows near Raveloe village, close to the edge of an isolated stone-pit. The Raveloe boys were both fascinated and intimidated by the objectionable sound produced by Silas's loom that was so unlike the cheerful, trotting noise of the winnowing-machine, or the easy rhythm of the flail. The village boys would often abandon their nutting or birds'-nesting to peep in at Silas's window, awestruck as they watched the strange action of the loom, its alternating noises

almost mocking them. They were greeted by an air of scornful superiority by the weaver, busy at work with a bent back and a treadmill attitude. But sometimes, when Marner paused momentarily to adjust his thread, he was aware of the presence of the scoundrels. He hated their intrusion so much that he would get down from his loom, open the door, and stare at them so fixedly that they would flee in terror.

It was difficult to believe that those large, brown and protruding eyes in Silas Marner's pale face did not see beyond normal human sight. Why, that dreadful gaze was also rumoured to cause rickets, cramps or a wry mouth in a boy! Their fathers and mothers had also told them that Silas Marner was capable of curing rheumatism if he had a mind, adding darkly that if one could speak the devil's language, he might save you the doctor's cost.

Fifteen years ago, Silas Marner had walked into Raveloe as a thin, young man. His brown eyes were short-sighted, and he appeared to be an average young man but for the strange peculiarities that went along with his exceptional vocation. To the villagers, Marner was as mysterious as one could get, hailing from an unknown region known as 'North'ard'. His lifestyle was strange too, as he invited no one inside his home, nor did he walk into the village to have a pint at the Rainbow. He never gossiped at the wheelwright's, sought no man or woman except when his profession demanded it, or when he needed supplies. The Raveloe lasses soon realised that Silas Marner would never coax one of them to accept him against her will. It was also as if he had heard them swear that they would never marry a dead man, who had returned to live again.

So, the years rolled by without the villagers changing their views about Marner, although they became more habituated to him. After fifteen years, the Raveloe men had the same things to say about Silas Marner as they did fifteen years earlier. True, they did not say these things that often, but they believed in what they said even more strongly now. Only one addition had been made in all these years: Master Marner had hidden away a lot of money somewhere, and was capable of buying up 'bigger men' than himself. Marner led a life of solitude over the years, and his habits remained unchanged.

But years ago, Marner was thought of very highly in a narrow religious sect that he belonged to. This small hidden world was known to itself as the church gathering in Lantern Yard. Marner was popular here and considered amongst the most faithful. Marner had inherited the knowledge of a few medicinal herbs, and the secret of their preparation. But Marner had grown skeptical about the use of this knowledge lately, concluding that herbs could not work magic without prayers. Hence, the inherited joy of wandering the fields in

search of foxglove, dandelion, and coltsfoot was abandoned as Marner perceived this to be a temptation.

A young man was among the members of this church, a little older than Marner. The two had become such close friends that the Lantern Yard brethren called them David and Jonathan. William Dane was the real name of this friend, and he was also considered as the epitome of youthful devotion, albeit sometimes severe towards weaker brethren. He was also perceived to be dazzled by his own light, to consider himself wiser than his masters. But in Marner's eyes, he was perfect and without fault, as the inexperienced Marner possessed a self-doubting nature that admired urgency and refutation.

This friendship remained unaffected even after Silas formed an attachment with a young servant-woman. Marner was engaged to Sarah, only waiting for an increase in their mutual savings before he married her. Marner was

delighted that Sarah never objected to William being present in their Sunday meetings. Then, a senior deacon fell seriously ill. As he was a childless widower, he was tended to night and day by the younger brethren and sisters. Silas and William often took their turn in this night-watch, one relieving the other at two in the morning. The old deacon was on the way to recovery, surprising everyone, when Silas sat up by his bedside one day to realise that his breathing had stopped. He examined the patient to realise that he had been dead for some time. 'Was I asleep?' Silas asked himself, and saw that it was four in the morning. But where was William? Why hadn't he turned up?

An anxious Marner ran to seek help, and soon many friends gathered along with the minister. Silas left for work, and at six o' clock, he was thinking of going to find William, when he arrived accompanied by the minister. They took Silas to Lantern Yard, where the minister displayed a pocket-knife to Silas, as everybody watched him. 'Do you know where you had left your knife?' the minister enquired. Silas replied that he was unaware that it had been outside his own pocket, although he was shaking at this strange interrogation. 'Do not hide your sin! Confess and repent instead!' he was urged. The knife had been discovered near the bedside of the dead deacon. It rested where the small bag of church money had been. It was missing and it was only logical that the owner of the knife had stolen it. 'God will clear my name!' an astonished Silas replied. 'I know nothing about the money or the knife going there. Search me and my house. You will find nothing but three pound five of my savings. William Dane is aware that I have them for six months.'

William groaned at this statement, and the minister said. 'Brother Marner, the proof weighs heavily against you. The money was taken last night, and there was no one there except you. William Dane has declared that a sudden sickness prevented his going there to take his usual place. You said yourself that he had not come, and you neglected the dead body as well.'

'I must have slept off,' Marner protested. 'The thief must have arrived and left while I was asleep.'

Marner's dwelling was searched, and William Dane discovered the bag there, tucked away behind the chest of drawers in Silas's chambers.

'Confess! Do not hide your sin any longer!' William pleaded with Silas now.

'You have known me for nine years, William,' Silas stated with a look of reproach. 'Have you known me to lie ever? But God will clear me!'

'Brother, how do I know what you have done in the secret chambers of your heart, to help Satan win you over?' William replied. Silas was

shocked and trembled. 'I remember now,' he said faintly. 'The knife was not in my pocket!'

'I do not know what you mean,' William declared. But Silas offered no explanation when others enquired where the knife had been.

'God will clear me!' was all Silas said.

Silas Marner was pronounced guilty and suspended from church membership. He was asked to give up the stolen money, and only if he confessed to his sins and repented for them, would he be readmitted to the church. Marner listened silently, and then addressed William Dane, 'I remember using my knife last, when I cut a strap for you. I don't recall putting it in my pocket again. You stole the money, and have plotted to frame me. But you might prosper despite your sins as there is no God that rules the world in a righteous manner. The God of Lies rules, bearing witness against the innocent.'

Everyone shook at this blasphemy.

'I leave our brethren to judge the voice of Satan,' William replied meekly. 'I can only pray for you Silas.'

A broken and dejected Marner returned home, and sat there for an entire day, stunned to silence. He had no desire to approach Sarah and convince her of his innocence. He started work in his loom on the second day, and hours later, the minister and a deacon brought him a message from Sarah. She had ended their engagement. Silas turned away and got back to work. Sarah married William Dane a month later, and Silas Marner left town soon after.

Chapter Two

The Lonesome Miser

Silas Marner had arrived to reside in Raveloe, leaving behind his own country and people. This low, woody region was so unlike his native place, that was within view of widespread hills. Here, he felt hidden from the very heavens, thanks to the trees and hedgerows. When he awoke in the morning, all he could sight were the dewy brambles and rank tufted grass.

To relieve himself from the rude shock that had made him leave his hometown, Marner weaved like a madman in his loom. He worked late into the night to finish Mrs. Osgood's table-linen, before it was expected to be finished. He did not think even once about the money that she would give him for the work, and weaved mechanically, just like a spider, from pure impulse and without thought. It was a classic example as to how a man's work, engaged in a steadfast manner, becomes an end in itself. His work bridged the loveless chasms of Silas Marner's life.

Silas's hand was content in throwing the shuttle, and his eye was satisfied to sight the little squares in the cloth get completed. Time was further killed by preparing his own food, fetching his water from the well, and putting his kettle on the fire. Thus, Silas's life was reduced to the meticulous routine of a spinning insect. He dismissed the thought of the past from his mind, and no feelings of companionship were stirred in him when he met strangers. The future appeared dark as no one cared for him. Any affection that might have existed in his heart was buried by the bruise inflicted upon him.

Silas was paid in gold when he finished Mrs. Osgood's table-linen. This was in stark contrast to his native town, where his earnings had been on a weekly basis, and lesser in comparison. Also, a major share of his earnings in his native place had been consumed by piety and charity. But now, he had more money in the form of five bright guineas, but nothing to spend it on. What need does a man have for guineas if he spent all day weaving in a loom? But it was good to feel them in his palm all the same, and stare at their bright faces. Silas had loved the purpose of money before, but now, the purpose had disappeared.

Slowly and steadily, the guineas, crowns and the half-crowns grew to a considerable heap as Marner's needs became simpler each day. All that dominated his thoughts was how to keep himself strong enough to work sixteen hours a day. But it was a strange satisfaction for Marner

to see the heaps of ten grow into a square, and then to a larger square. Each added guinea was added satisfaction for Silas, breeding a new sense of desire that egged him on. This world was a strange, hopeless riddle for the weaver, and he might have weaved endlessly till he forgot totally about the riddle. But the money had arrived to mark off his weaving into periods, and although the money grew, it was saved and not consumed.

Marner held the coins in his fingers, handling them and counting them till his thirst was quenched, and he was fully satisfied with the experience. This was only in the night when he had finished his work, and they were like companions in the night. In his floor underneath his room, Silas had created a hole in which he placed his iron pot with his guineas and silver coins, covering it with bricks. The bricks were covered with sand whenever coins were replaced.

Years went by and Silas lived a life of solitude. The guineas in the iron pot increased, and his life narrowed down to reach a hardness seldom experienced by any living being. His life had been restricted now to just weaving and hoarding, without any thought of how these functions would culminate. His face and figure shrank and bent just like a mechanical object, to resemble a crooked tube or handle that was devoid of any meaning in terms of appearance. The once prominent eyes were reduced to tiny grains and he became withered and yellow. Even though he was not yet forty, the children called him 'Old Master Marner'.

This is Silas Marner's history, after fifteen years of life in Raveloe. After working monotonously and mechanically by the day, he indulged in revelry with his gold at night. The iron pot could not hold the coins anymore and two thick leather bags had been fashioned to do the needful. Silas saved the gold and chose the

silver to attend to his bodily wants, spending shillings and sixpences mostly. Silas loved all his coins, considering the guineas as his unborn children. But during Christmas that fifteenth year, Silas Marner's life experienced a second great change. His history blended in a singular way with the life of his neighbours.

Chapter Three

Godfrey's Secret

Squire Cass was the greatest man in Raveloe. He lived in a big red house almost opposite the church that boasted of a beautiful flight of stone steps in front and high stables behind it. Squire Cass was one of the many landed parishioners, but only he held the honourable title of Squire. Although Mr. Osgood's family origins were probably as old, he just owned the farm he lived in. In contrast, Squire Cass also had a few tenants.

The Squire's wife had died long ago and the Red House did not have a mother or wife that is a must if kitchen and parlour have to flourish with love. This perhaps explained the lack of order and discipline in his house, and why his sons looked ill. Moral censure was not severe in a place like Raveloe, but the Squire was perceived to be weak as he had kept all his sons sitting idle at home. People shook their heads in disapproval at the acts of the second son Dunstan, known as Dunsey Cass.

Dunsey was a compulsive better and swopper in addition to being a spiteful jeering chap. He seemed to relish his drink even more when other people went dry. Dunsey ensured that he was careful in his exploits so that they did not bring disrepute to a family like Squire Cass's that owned a monument in the church and tankards older than King George himself. But it was a pity that Mr. Godfrey, the eldest son should take the same road as his brother, as he was doing of late. Mr. Godfrey was a fine, good-natured young man, and would surely lose Miss Nancy Lammeter if he continued this way. It was well known that she had chosen to look shyly on him lately. But there was talk in town when Mr. Godfrey was away from home for many days without anyone knowing where he'd been. There was also something odd about him upon his return; he didn't look as fresh as before and the colour had drained from his face. 'What a perfect couple Mr. Godfrey and Miss Lammeter would make!' was the general statement at one time. If Miss Nancy Lammeter became the mistress of the Red House, it would be a fine change indeed! The Lammeters had been raised in such a manner that they never permitted even a pinch of salt to be wasted, and yet everyone in their household lacked for nothing. Having such a daughter-in-law would be a blessing for the old Squire. But if Mr. Godfrey did not mend his ways, he might have to say goodbye to Miss Lammeter.

One late November afternoon, in Silas Marner's fifteenth year at Raveloe, the once hopeful Godfrey stood in his dark parlour with his hands in his pockets and his back to the fire. The walls were adorned with guns, whips, and foxes' brushes, and coats and hats were flung about on the chairs. The fire was half-choked, with pipes stacked up against the chimney-corners. The signs were evocative of a domestic life that lacked charm. The look of gloominess on Godfrey's face was perhaps the nail in the coffin. He appeared to be waiting for someone, and the sound of a heavy step, followed by a whistle was heard across the huge entrance hall.

The door opened to admit a man heavy in appearance and his flushed, elated face bore the first stage of intoxication. At the sight of Dunsey, Godfrey's face shed its expression of gloom and was replaced with hatred. The good looking brown spaniel reclining on the hearth retreated under the safety of the chair in the chimney corner.

'Master Godfrey!' Dunsey stated mockingly. 'Well, what is it you want with me? You are my elder after all and I was bound to come when you asked for me.'

'Just shake yourself sober and listen to what I have to tell you,' Godfrey retaliated in a savage manner. He had himself been drinking more than he ought to, in an attempt to convert his melancholy into rage. 'I called to tell you that I must hand over Fowler's rent to the Squire, or tell him that I gave you that money. He has been threatening to send word to Cox to distrain for the money and it'll be known soon, regardless of the fact that I tell him or not. He shall do what he threatens to do, if Fowler doesn't pay up his dues by this week. You know the Squire's short of cash. So he won't take any nonsense. You know what he threatened to do to you if he discovered you taking away his money again, don't you? Get the money and get it quickly!'

'Ah!' Dunsey sneered, as he approached his brother and looked him straight in the face. 'What if you get the money yourself and save me the trouble? If you were so kind to give it to me in the first place, surely you will be kind enough to pay it back for me as well? Where's your brotherly love now?'

Godfrey bit his lip, and clenched his fists in rage. 'I'll knock you down if you give me that look,' he threatened Dunsey.

'No, no. You won't do that,' Dunsey stated, moving away quickly though. 'I'm such a good-natured brother, you see. Otherwise, I could have had you thrown out of your house with your inheritance cut off. Why, I might just tell the Squire how his favourite son was married to that nice, young woman named Molly Farren. Why, I can easily tell him why his dear son couldn't live with his alcoholic wife. I could

then easily slip into your place and live in comfort while he throws you out. But good man that I am, I haven't done it. You should therefore share my troubles too. Get that hundred pounds for me! I know you will!'

'But how can I?' Godfrey said, almost shaking. 'I don't have a single shilling to save myself. You can't take my place and you know it. You'd get thrown out too, as if you start tattling tales, I shall follow.'

'Oh, never mind,' Dunsey declared. 'Although we quarrel all the time, I don't know what I'd do without you, my handsome brother! But I know that there's nothing better you'd like than for the both of us to stay at home together. So, get me that money and I'll say goodbye, although I must say that I'm sorry to be parting from you.'

Godfrey rushed after a departing Dunstan, and restrained him, by holding his arm. 'I have no money!' he said with an oath. 'I tell you that I can't get any money.'

'Borrow of old Kimble.'

'He won't lend me any more money. I shan't ask him.'

'Sell Wildfire, then.'

'That's easier said. I must have the money directly.'

'All you have to do is to ride him to the hunt tomorrow. Bryce and Keating will be there surely. You'll get more bids than one.'

'I have to attend Mrs. Osgood's birthday dance tomorrow,' Godfrey declared.

'Oho!' Dunsey exclaimed, cocking his head to a side and attempting to speak in a small mincing treble. 'Sweet Miss Nancy will be coming and we shall dance with her. We shall promise never to be naughty again and...'

'Hold your tongue, you fool!' Godfrey turned red and exclaimed angrily. 'Say another word about her and I'll throttle you.'

'Why?' Dunsey said, picking up a whip from the table and beating its butt end on his palm. 'You stand a good chance with her. My advice would be to attach yourself to her sleeve again. It would be saving time. If Molly should take a drop too much of laudanum one day, that would make you a widower. Miss Nancy wouldn't mind being a second wife if she didn't know about it, would she? You know you've got a good-natured brother who can keep your secret if you help him out.'

'My patience has reached its end,' Godfrey declared. 'You push a man too far. I might just tell the Squire everything myself. That might help me get you off my back, if nothing else. He is bound to know about it sometime or the other, anyway. Molly has been threatening to do so herself. So don't flatter yourself to think that the secret you keep has a price attached to it. You have drained me of money so I can't keep her quiet. So you can go to the devil!'

Dunsey realised that he had stretched things too far. But he said casually, 'As you wish. I

think I'll have a draught of ale first,' he said and rang the bell. Then, throwing himself across two chairs, he rapped the window seat with his whip handle. Godfrey stood uncertainly, hands in pockets and back to the fire. His big, muscular body had plenty of raw courage. But when it came to taking a big decision under pressure, this animal courage was of no help. These dangers could not be knocked down with the fist or throttled with brute force. The more Godfrey considered being reduced to the disinherited son of a squire and having to beg and dig, the more upsetting it was to him. He was as helpless as an uprooted tree that had grown into a handsome bulk, shooting upwards with help from the earth and the sky.

Perhaps the loss of inheritance would have been justified if it meant having Nancy by his side. But that would never be as he would lose her as well, if he lost the inheritance. The only option left for him would be to enlist as a

soldier, with the fear of death always present. Respectable families perceived taking up of a soldier's profession as a step that was most desperate, just short of suicide. No! Godfrey thought. It was better to live this life, drinking the wine he loved and feasting like a king. The sale of his horse seemed the only solution to the problem. But he would not give in before a final quarrel.

'Only you could have suggested selling Wildfire in that cool manner,' Godfrey burst out in anger and bitterness. 'He is the last thing I can call my own and the best horse I ever possessed. You have no pride in you to see the stables emptied in this manner and everybody sneering about it. I think you are well capable to sell yourself off to make someone feel as if he'd got a bad bargain.'

'Yes, I see you do me justice,' Dunsey replied. 'I'm an ace when it comes to pushing people into bargains. Allow me to sell Wildfire

for you for that very reason. Let me ride him to the hunt tomorrow. Of course, I shall not look as handsome as the owner. But they shall bid for the horse and not the rider.'

'Trust my horse to you?' Godfrey said in disgust.

'As you wish!' Dunsey said calmly. 'It's you who has to pay Fowler's money as it is no business of mine. The Squire knows you have it. You chose to give it to me. It's nothing to me if you pay up or not. I just offered to sell your horse for you as you are busy tomorrow.'

Godfrey considered the situation silently for some time. What he would like to do was to jump on his brother, snatch the whip and flog him mercilessly. But he knew he had to give in.

'You'll sell the horse and hand over the money?' he demanded. 'If you don't, everything will go down. Your own skull will be broken with mine.'

'Yes, yes,' Dunsey said, rising to his feet. 'I

knew you'd see reason. I'll get you a hundred twenty for that horse.'

'Make sure you are sober tomorrow,' Godfrey warned. 'You might get pitched on your head tomorrow otherwise.'

Dunsey reassured his brother and slammed the door behind him as he left. Godfrey was left pondering over his strange personal circumstances. But what was promising was the party he had to attend. The sporting, drinking, card-playing, and the rare pleasure of seeing Nancy Lammeter again was something to look forward to.

Chapter Four

Dunsey's Theft

Dunstan Cass travelled in the hot morning sun and his path fell on the lane where Silas Marner's cottage stood. 'That old fool of a weaver must have a lot of money stashed away somewhere!' was Dunsey's first thought as he heard Silas rattling away. 'How come it never came to my mind to suggest to Godfrey that the old miser should be persuaded or frightened into parting with some of his money?' He thought. But then again, he wanted Godfrey to suffer, and he had a horse to sell. So, Dunsey continued with his journey.

Dunsey found Bryce and Keating just as he had expected; Bryce bought the horse for a hundred and twenty. This money was agreed to be paid after Wildfire was delivered at the Batherley stables. Dunsey knew he should give up the idea of a day's hunt and set off for Batherley immediately. After delivering Wildfire, he should hire a horse and ride home. But the urge for a run, encouraged at the successful negotiation and fuelled by a draught of brandy, made Dunsey push his luck. In his eagerness to impress the crowds, Dunsey made Wildfire jump a fence too many, and Wildfire was pierced by a hedge-stake. Dunsey escaped without any injuries but Wildfire painfully breathed his last.

The only reaction Dunsey had was that there had been no witnesses to this accident. His first thoughts were to reach Batherley from where he would hire a horse and go home. But to walk so many miles on a deserted road without a gun was not a good idea. But Dunsey had no other option as it was almost four o'clock, and a mist gathered. So, Dunsey set off for Raveloe instead, and after a long walk, the lights in the cottage of Silas Marner greeted his eyes. The thought of the old weaver and his hidden gold had been on Dunsey's mind throughout his walk, and he had been inventing ways as to how he could coax or force the weaver to part with his money.

Dunsey wasn't a man of force, and his plan was to trick the weaver into making him believe that his money would be repaid. The weaver was sure to have a spare lantern as well that Dunsey could use to reach home, which was still three quarters of a mile away. The mist had transformed into rain and the road was slippery and wet. Dunsey somehow managed to reach Marner's door in the dark and knocked loudly, relishing the fact that it could scare the miserly weaver. But there was no answer and the cottage was silent. Had the weaver gone to

sleep, then? But then, why hadn't he switched off the light? That was strange for a miser! Dunsey knocked loudly again, and then pushed his fingers through the latch-hole. He wanted to shake the door and pull the latch-string up and down to get the miser's attention.

To Dunsey's surprise, the door opened and he found himself in front of a fire that burned brightly. Everything in the cottage was lit up, but the weaver was absent. Dunsey instantly seated himself by the inviting fire, where something was cooking. A small portion of pork was suspended from the kettle hanger by a string that passed through a large door key. The pork had been hung at some distance from the fire, so that it didn't roast too quickly during the weaver's absence.

'So, the miser has hot meat for supper?' Dunsey thought. 'People said he lived on mouldy bread to check his appetite. Well, they were so wrong. But where is the miser, leaving

his supper here, and his door unlocked? Maybe he has gone to fetch fuel? Or maybe he has slipped into the stone-pit?'

The last thought appealed particularly to Dunsey. 'But if the weaver died, who would receive his money?' he thought again. Then, one pressing question dominated his thoughts. 'Where is the money?'

Dunsey's mind was dull, but even that dull mind knew that there were only three possible places where cottagers hoarded their money: the thatch, the bed, and a hole in the floor. The weaver's cottage did not have a thatch, and Dunsey went up to the bed immediately. But as he did so, his eyes travelled sharply over the floor. He saw the bricks distinctly under the sprinkling of sand. But one spot arrested his attention, as it was covered entirely with sand. This sand also had the mark of fingers over it, carefully spreading it over a particular space. This spot was close to the treddles of the loom,

and Dunsey rushed there immediately. Using his whip, he swept the sand away. He inserted the thin end of the hook between the bricks, to discover they were loose. He lifted up two bricks and his eyes lit up to spot two leather bags. Their weight suggested that they were filled with guineas.

Dunsey ensured that there were no more bags by feeling around the hole. Then he speedily replaced the bricks and spread sand over them. Only five minutes had elapsed since he had entered the cottage, but it seemed like an eternity to Dunsey, who was a little frightened now. The rain and the darkness had thickened, and this made Dunsey glad, even though it would be cumbersome walking with both hands full. Dunsey quickly stepped outside the cottage and into the darkness.

Chapter Five

Silas Marner is Robbed

Silas Marner was just a hundred yards from his cottage when Dunsey left it. He moved slowly, armed with a horn lantern, making his way from the village, using a sack around his shoulders as an overcoat. He was tired but his mind was peaceful. Silas thought about his hot supper which was particularly good as it was free of cost. The pork was a gift from Miss Priscilla Lammeter to whom he had delivered a handsome linen piece. It was because of such a present that Silas indulged in such a good meal.

But after knotting his string around the piece of pork, it struck Silas that the piece of twine was essential for his work the next morning. It was a nasty fog he had to step into to fetch the twine from the village. The errand in normal weather would have consumed only twenty minutes, but now took longer. The door could not be locked without undoing the well-knotted string that was instrumental in slow heating his supper. Besides, which thief would dare to venture outdoors on a storm like this? Especially as none had come for fifteen years!

Silas reached his cottage and immediately set about warming himself and tending the pork at the same time. Even though most people in Raveloe regarded Silas with contemptuous pity, fear, and even suspicion, he was actually a harmless man. Even though he had become avaricious in nature to the amount of actually worshipping gold, he was never harmful to others. He worked for his money honestly. His obsession demanded that he have a look at his precious guineas before his meal. It would be a pleasure to see them as he feasted, actually. Joy is the best wine, after all, and Silas's guineas were like golden wine.

Silas did not notice any change as he swept away the sand to remove the bricks. But his heart missed a beat as he sighted the empty hole. The feeling that his gold was missing did not register at first. He was consumed by panic and the eager effort to end the terror. His hand trembled as he held the candle to inspect the hole repeatedly. Then he shook so violently that the candle fell. He held his hands to his head, trying to steady himself. Was it possible that he had kept the gold somewhere else and forgotten all about it?

Silas trembled as he got up to look at the table. Wasn't the gold there? Silas searched everywhere in the cottage in vain. His eyes saw every object, except the missing bags. He put his hands to his head, and let out a terrible scream; a wild, desolate cry. He stood motionless for a

while after that, but the cry had relieved some of the initial pressure of the harsh truth. He turned to stagger towards his loom and got into his working seat. This instinctive action helped him get a strong grip of reality. False hopes had disappeared now and the first shock of being certain was a thing of the past. The thought that the thief could be caught and the gold might be restored was entertained eagerly by Silas now. He opened his door and the heavy rain descended upon him. No footsteps could be traced on such a night. But when had the thief come? Was it a thief or some cruel power that gained pleasure in reducing him to such a state for the second time?

Silas considered the people who could be responsible for the theft. There was Jem Rodney, a known poacher. He had often encountered Silas on the fields and had made comments in jest about the weaver's hidden money. Jem was the culprit! He had to return the gold.

Silas would not punish him if he did so. Silas thought about going and reporting his loss to the great men in the village like the constable, the clergyman, and Squire Cass. They would make Jem or whoever the thief was, cough up the stolen money. Silas ran out in the rain, not even bothering to protect himself, or lock the door. Hadn't he lost everything? He ran like a madman till he was near the Rainbow at the village entrance.

The Rainbow, according to Silas, was the haven of rich and stout husbands. Their wives had a surplus of linen, and the important people of Raveloe were to be found here. Silas could easily and swiftly make his loss public here. But the parlour was dark tonight as all the eminent personalities were at Mrs. Osgood's birthday dance. There was a hush inside as Silas Marner entered and scrutinised the company with his strange, inhuman eyes. The long silence was finally broken by the landlord, who felt he had a business to protect.

'Master Marner, what's your business here?' he asked gently.

'Robbed! I've been robbed,' Silas gasped. 'I want the constable, and the Justice. I want Squire Cass and Mr. Crackenthorp.'

'Get a hold on him, Jem Rodney,' the landlord said. 'He's gone off his head.'

Jem Rodney sat close to where Silas stood, but refused to do the needful.

'Do it yourself, Mr. Snell,' Jem stated. 'He's been robbed, and murdered too.'

'Jem Rodney!' Silas exclaimed, setting his eyes on his suspect.

'Aye, Master Marner, what is it you want with me?' Jem asked, trembling a bit. He grabbed his drinking can defensively.

'If you stole my money,' Silas said pleadingly, 'give it back and I won't set the constable on you. I'll let you have a guinea.'

'Me stole your money?' Jem replied angrily. 'I'll throw this can at your eye if you call me a thief again.'

The landlord intervened, making Silas take off his coat and having him sit on a chair in the centre of the circle, and in direct line of the fire. Silas Marner told them everything and they were convinced that he was telling the truth now.

'Jem Rodney hasn't committed this crime, Master Marner,' the landlord said. 'He's been sitting here drinking much before you left your house.'

'Yes, one cannot accuse the innocent,' Mr. Macey stated. Silas apologised to Jem as he realised this was true.

'How much money was there in the bags, Master Marner?'

'Two hundred and seventy-two pounds, twelve and sixpence, when I counted it last night,' Silas groaned and replied.

It was decided that two men would go with Silas to Kench, the constable's house, as he was sick and in bed. So, the landlord and Mr. Dowlas accompanied Silas to Kench's house.

Chapter Six

Godfrey Arrives at a Decision

Godfrey Cass returned from Mrs. Osgood's party at midnight, and it did not surprise him at all that Dunsey hadn't returned home yet. Maybe he had been unable to sell Wildfire, and was awaiting another chance to do so. It was a foggy afternoon when he had left, and he might have chosen to lodge at the Red Lion at Batherley to spend the night. Godfrey's mind was also full of thoughts about Nancy Lammeter to give much thought either to his horse or his brother.

The next morning, the news of the robbery at the weaver's house spread like wildfire throughout the village. Godfrey was also no exception when it came to discussing the events, and visiting the Stone-pits. The rain had washed away any footprints that the thief might have left behind, but a close inspection of the spot revealed something rather interesting. A tinderbox with a flint and steel had been found in the direction opposite the village, half sunk in the mud. This did not belong to Silas, as the tinderbox he owned stood on his shelf. So, the general impression was that this tinderbox had a connection with the robbery.

There were some who did not believe that the tinderbox was connected with the robbery, and some thought that Marner's tale was a queer one. Godfrey, however, had lost his interest in the robbery as thoughts of Wildfire and Dunstan consumed him now. 'Could it be that Dunstan had run off with Wildfire?' He thought alarmingly. The possibility that Dunstan would return after a month after gambling away all the proceeds of the horse was also a frightening one. Godfrey was angry with himself for entrusting his horse to Dunstan.

Suddenly, Godfrey heard a horse approach. But his heart sank when he saw it was not Wildfire. It was Bryce, and not Dunstan, who pulled up to talk to him. Bryce did not look very agreeable.

'Mr. Godfrey, that brother of yours, Master Dunsey, is a lucky man, isn't he?'

'What do you mean?' Godfrey asked quickly.

'Hasn't he reached home yet?'

'No! What has happened to him? Tell me quickly. What has he done with my horse?' Godfrey demanded.

'Ah, I had assumed it was yours, although he said that you had given it to him.'

'Has the horse thrown him off? Has he broken his knees?'

'Worse than that,' Bryce replied. 'I had made

an offer of a hundred and twenty for that horse. It was a good price! But what does he do after that? He flies at a hedge with stakes in it, on top of a bank, with a ditch ahead. He stakes that horse and kills it!'

'He'd better stay away from me,' Godfrey said angrily. 'I've been such a fool to entrust my horse to his care.'

'Well, the truth is that I suspected that he might be selling your horse without your knowledge. I know Master Dunsey's tricks. I wonder where he's disappeared. I'm sure he is unhurt as he has walked away.'

'He shall never be hurt,' Godfrey said bitterly. 'All he can do is hurt others.'

'So you did give him the permission to sell your horse, then?' Bryce enquired.

'Yes, I did,' Godfrey admitted, his pride hurt that his lack of money was revealed to Bryce. Godfrey parted from Bryce, riding slowly, thinking about the confrontation with his father

that was no longer avoidable. The revelation about the money had to be declared the next morning itself. If Dunstan returned and told all, his father's wrath would be severe. One thing could be done. If he told his father that he had spent the money instead of Dunstan, the matter would blow over after a little storm. This was because Godfrey had never committed such an offence before like Dunstan had.

Godfrey realised that if he let this opportunity of confession slip by, he would perhaps never have another. Molly might just arrive as she had threatened to do. Godfrey tried to relax by rehearsing what he would eventually tell his father. The old Squire was an unappeasable man, and made decisions in violent anger. Even after his rage had subsided later, he could not be swayed from those decisions. He was just like fiery volcanic material that hardened to rock even after cooling. Like many violent men, he permitted evils to grow, till they were

monstrous. Then he crushed those evils with relentless force and this was the system he followed with his tenants. He let them get into arrears and go the wrong way as the case may be, and would crush them with the strongest measures, showing no mercy.

Godfrey was worried about this nature of his father, and when he woke up the next morning, he was more nervous than before. Godfrey decided that he had viewed the matter in a wrong light the day before. His rage for Dunstan had clouded his thoughts. Instead of confessing to his father and cutting all his hopes, he would soften his father's rage against Dunsey, and keep things just the way they were.

Chapter Seven

The Weaver's Plight

Justice Malam was considered in Tarley and Raveloe as a man in possession of a voluminous mind. This was because he was capable of detection without evidence unlike the members of the Commission of the Peace. Surely, such a man would not dismiss the tinderbox as a clue. But weeks went by, and there was no success in the investigation of the robbery. The excitement the robbery had caused in Raveloe gradually subsided. Duncan Cass's absence was hardly perceived as suspicious as the young man was often prone to leaving after a quarrel with his father. But no one connected the fact that

Dunsey had disappeared on the very same day of the robbery at Marner's cottage.

Poor Silas was devastated. The loom was there and so was the weaving. But his treasure had disappeared, and every now and then, he moaned in pain while weaving. Throughout the evening, Silas sat by the fire, his elbows on his knees, clasping his head with both hands. He moaned in a low monotone, like someone who does not wish to be heard. But he was not deserted in his hour of trouble. The neighbours who had always been repulsed by Marner, pitied him now. The fact that a cunning man like Silas Marner had been cheated off his money, evoked sympathy. This change of attitude was reflected by kind acts towards the weaver.

The odour of Christmas cooking was in the air. This was the season when well-off families engaged in charity by distributing pork and black pudding to the less fortunate. Housekeepers like Mrs. Osgood cooked for

Silas and Mr. Crackenthrop, who was of the view that Silas Marner had been robbed because he never came to Church, gifted him pigs' pettitoes. Neighbours who had nothing to give, offered verbal consolation when they met Silas in the village. People started calling on him at his cottage to discuss his misfortune, cheered him up and offered their sympathies.

Mrs. Winthrop, the wheelwright's wife, also tried to convince Silas to attend Church. This woman was naturally drawn to those who suffered. She was also the first person everyone in Raveloe thought of whenever there was an illness or death in a family, whenever leeches had to be applied, or when a monthly nurse failed in her duties. She was a grave, kind, serious, good-looking woman who did not whimper, cry or possess a temper. It seemed strange that Ben Winthrop, a man who loved his joke and quart-pot, got along so well with Dolly. Mrs. Winthrop took her husband's joviality and

jokes as patiently as all her other duties. It could be said that she perceived the stronger sex to be somewhat like animals, naturally troublesome like bulls and turkey-cocks.

But despite the persuasions of Dolly Winthrop and Mr. Macey, Silas spent a lonely Christmas Day. He ate his meat sadly and the evening snowfall made him even gloomier. He sat there in his house, moaning, not bothering to lock his doors or close the shutters. When the cold grabbed him, he realised that his fire was grey. In contrast, the bells in Raveloe village rang merrily and the Church was totally full. No one mentioned Dunstan at Squire Cass's family party and no one was sorry that he was absent.

But the Christmas day party was restricted only to family. The great dance on New Year's Eve was the big event hosted by Squire Cass at the Red House. It was a tradition of sorts from his forefathers' times. This was the event when all of the society of Raveloe and

Tarley assembled together. Fair dames arrived on pillions, sending their bandboxes before them, supplied with more than their evening costumes. The plentiful feast that was spread out was the talk of the town and did not end in just one evening. Godfrey Cass was looking forward to this New Year's Eve with a foolish expectation. He did not even pay heed to his best friend called Anxiety.

'Dunsey will come home soon and there will be a great blow-up,' Anxiety whispered into Godfrey's ear. 'How will you bribe his silence then?'

'Oh, he won't come home before New Year's Eve,' Godfrey replied. 'I shall sit by Nancy then and dance with her.'

'But money is needed now,' Anxiety said loudly. 'How will you get that money without selling your mother's diamond pin? If you don't get that money…'

'Something will happen to make things easier,' Godfrey stated. 'At least there is one

pleasure for me close at hand. Nancy is coming!'

'What if your father brings matters to such an event that you cannot marry her?'

'Hold your tongue, I say! Don't worry me. I can see Nancy's eyes as they will look into mine. I can feel her hand in mine already.'

But Anxiety was not convinced and went on and on all through the noisy Christmas crowd. It refused to be quiet despite much drinking and revelry.

Chapter Eight

The Strange Visitor

While Godfrey Cass was at the dance, forgetting his troubles in Nancy's sweet presence, his wife Molly was walking with slow, unsure steps through the Raveloe lanes that were totally snow covered. She was carrying her child in her arms. This journey on New Year's Eve was a predetermined one for her. This was her act of vengeance that she had kept buried in her heart ever since Godfrey had declared that he would rather die than acknowledge her as his better half.

Molly was well aware that there would be a spectacular party at the Red House on New Year's Eve. Her husband would be the cynosure

of all eyes there, and she was determined to spoil his pleasure there. She would do this by paying him a visit dressed in her dingy rags, her once beautiful face, now faded, carrying her child that had its father's hair and eyes. She would present herself to the Squire as his eldest son's wife and the mother of his child.

Molly was also aware that the reason for her dingy rags was not her husband's neglect but her opium addiction. Molly was a slave of opium, body and soul. But her mother's heart refused to relinquish her hungry child to her husband. Molly was bitter towards Godfrey because she felt that it was her right to be well-off just like her husband. The fact that Godfrey repented marrying her and she suffered because of this act, only served to increase her bitterness towards her husband.

She had set off rather early, but had lingered on the road thinking in her laziness that the snow would stop falling if she took shelter

under a warm shed. She waited in vain for a long time and her spirits fell considerably during this wait. It was seven o'clock and though she was very near Raveloe, she did not realise this since she was not familiar with the lanes that all looked the same. She sought comfort in the only thing she found comfort in; the black demon tucked away at her bosom. She raised it to her lips after a moment's hesitation. Her mother's love begged for painful consciousness but she would rather have pleasurable oblivion at this hour. Molly flung away something after a while. It was an empty phial!

Then she walked on again, drowsily clutching the sleeping child at her bosom. The demon worked his black magic slowly, aided by cold and tiredness. Soon Molly desired for nothing else but to lie down and sleep. She lay down against a bush that served as her pillow and the snow acted as a soft bed. It

did not matter to her that the bed was cold or that her child might wake up and cry for her. She still clutched on to the child instinctively, and the child still slept. But when her fingers relaxed finally, the blue eyes of the child opened. There was a little cry of 'mammy', which was not returned by the now deaf and numb mother.

The child was wet with snow, and as it rolled downwards on its mother's knees, its eyes caught a bright light. Its eyes were fixed on the bright thing approaching it, yet never arriving. The child decided it must catch that gleam and crawled on all fours, stretching out one hand to catch the gleam. But the gleam refused to be caught. So the little one decided to approach the gleam and crawled through the snow to the open door of Silas Marner's cottage. The child went to the warm hearth where a bright fire blazed. The little one put out its tiny hands towards

the fire and gurgled in contentment at the warmth. Then it went to sleep.

Although Silas was in the cottage, he hadn't seen the child enter. He was too absorbed thinking about his lost money. He had been told by someone that sitting up to usher in the New Year today was supposed to bring in good luck, and his money might be returned to him. So, that's what he was doing, although this was nothing but a Raveloe jest with a strange miser. Silas soon grew tired of standing, and seated himself on his fireside chair. He was about to push the logs together when he saw gold on the top of the hearth. Gold! It was his own gold that had returned as mysteriously as it had left.

His heart beat like a drum and he froze for a while. The heap of gold appeared to glow and grow larger under Silas's gaze. Silas finally stretched out his hands that met soft warm curls instead of hard coins. Silas was stunned to discover that it was a sleeping child that

his hands had touched. It was a fair, round child, with soft yellow rings on the head. Was it a strange dream? How had the child entered his cottage? And when? These thoughts were as strange to the weaver as old, irreconcilable friendships. It occurred to Silas that the child was a message from that far-off life, and he was overawed by the thought that some strange Power controlled his life. Silas concluded that the arrival of the child was magical and not a natural event.

A cry on the hearth indicated that the child was awake and Silas bent to lift it on his knee. The child clung around his neck and burst into cries of 'mammy', by which small children express their surprise on waking up. Silas pressed the child against him, hushing tender words. Silas fed the child some porridge sweetened with sugar and this stopped her crying. She stared quietly and widely at Silas. Then she slipped down from his knee and

began to toddle about the room. Silas followed her, so that she wouldn't fall against anything and hurt herself. But the child only fell to a sitting position and pulled at her boots, to denote with a crying face that they hurt her little feet. It was some time before it registered in Silas's mind that the boots caused her discomfort and he pulled them off with some difficulty.

The child chuckled and inspected the mystery of her own toes, inviting Silas to think about the mystery too. But the wet boots finally indicated to the weaver that the child had been walking on the snow and gave him the idea how she might have entered his house. He raised the child in his arms and approached the door. He saw her tiny marks on the snow.

'Mammy!' the child cried again and again, almost escaping from Silas's arms. Silas saw a human body on the snow. The head was sunk low and half-covered by the white snow.

Chapter Nine

A Dead Woman

It was after early supper had ended at the Red House. The entertainment that existed in this particular stage comprised bashfulness converted into easy and natural jollity. Gentlemen, normally reserved and conscious, could be prevailed upon now to dance a hornpipe. This was a time when the Squire chose to talk loudly, scattering snuff in the process, and slapping his visitors on the back. It was a time when people lingered longer on the whist-table, and this choice was exasperating to a man like Uncle Kimble. This was because he was a sober man, who became bitter and intense over brandy and cards.

Godfrey stood apart from the crowd, largely to keep Nancy in his sight, who was seated in a group, close to her father. The reason he wanted to be aloof was not to be subject to his father's jokes about marriage and to observe Nancy's beauty from a distance. He would have the chance of dancing with her once the hornpipe was over, but now it was gratifying to steal long glances at her without being observed.

Suddenly, something interrupted Godfrey's line of vision, startling him as if it were an apparition that had risen from the dead. It was the sight of his own child, carried by that weaver, Silas Marner. That was his instant impression of course, as he hadn't set eyes on the child for a long time. When he thought he was probably mistaken regarding the child's identity, he observed Mr. Crackenthorp and Mr. Lammater approach Marner. Godfrey joined the two men instantly, as he was unable to conceal his astonishment at this strange turn of events. He wanted to hear every word that was said, but was conscious that he should keep his emotions under control, lest someone noticed his reaction. For, he was white-lipped and shaking nervously like a leaf. But all eyes in the room were on the weaver!

'What is this?' the Squire demanded angrily. 'What do you mean coming here in this way?'

'The doctor! I've come for the doctor,' Silas said instantly to Mr. Crackenthorp.

'What's the matter, Marner?' the rector demanded.

'A woman,' Silas spoke in a low tone, just as Godfrey arrived. 'I think she's dead in the snow at the Stone-Pits, near my house.'

Godfrey felt something stabbing in his heart, as a wave of terror went through him. What if Molly was still alive? This was an evil terror from a man whose happiness depended on duplicity.

'Hush, Marner,' Mr. Crackenthorp said. 'Go and wait in the hall. I'll get the doctor.'

He explained the matter to the Squire in whispers, 'Found a woman in the snow, and thinks she's dead. The news will shock the ladies. So say as little about it as possible. Better to tell them that a poor woman is sick from hunger and cold. I'll fetch Kimble.'

The ladies had gathered closer now, curious why the reclusive weaver had arrived there under such strange circumstances, carrying such a pretty child. The child was frightened and shy on seeing such a huge crowd under lights. She hid her face with a frown.

'Whose child is it?' the ladies asked Silas in unison as Nancy Lammeter asked Godfrey the same question, who wrung out the reply with considerable effort. 'I-I don't know- some poor woman found in the snow, I believe,' he said.

'You must leave the child here, Master Marner,' the good-natured Mrs. Kimble

suggested. However, she hesitated to make contact herself with the dingy clothes worn by the child. 'I'll tell one of the girls to fetch it,' she stated.

'No!' Silas protested. 'I can't part from it. It's come to me and I have the right to keep it.'

This feeling to keep the child was a revelation to Silas himself, as he had no direct intention about keeping the child a minute ago. Just when the child was about to be taken away from him, this was uttered on sudden impulse.

'Fetch me a pair of thick boots, Godfrey,' Uncle Kimble ordered. 'Someone fetch Dolly as she's the best woman to have around now. Where is Ben? He was here before supper. Has he left?'

The scared child was clinging on to Marner now, and crying for her mammy all the time. Godfrey returned with the boots, and as the child cried, he felt some nerve drawn tight inside him. He gladly offered to leave, and fetch Dolly Winthrop.

'Pooh! Send someone else,' Uncle Kimble stated, and rushed away with Marner. But Godfrey decided to go himself as he wanted to escape the sight of the child. He grabbed his hat and coat, but he left in such a rush that he wore his thin shoes.

Dolly urged him to return when they reached Marner's cottage together, as the young gentleman would get his feet wet. But Godfrey insisted that he would wait outside, and asked her to call him if she needed help. 'You have a good heart, sir,' Dolly stated, as she went inside. Godfrey was too nervous to feel any self-contempt at this praise he was undeserving of. He walked up and down, oblivious that he was plunging ankle-deep in snow. All he thought was about what was happening in the cottage, and its consequences on his future. He thought momentarily about accepting the consequences of his past deeds. He should accept his wife and child. But he was a coward who could not put his thoughts into action.

'If she is dead, then I can marry Nancy,' he thought selfishly. 'I shall be a good fellow in the future if that happens. I shall keep no secrets, and the child shall be taken care of. But what if she lives?' the dark thought cropped up in his heart.

After a wait that seemed endless, Mr. Kimble emerged from within the cottage. Godfrey rushed forth to meet his uncle. 'I decided to wait for you, as I had travelled so far,' he explained quickly.

'Pooh! It was silly on your part to come out. Why didn't you send one of your men? The woman's dead! Been dead for hours, I should say.'

'What sort of woman is she?' Godfrey asked, as the colour returned to his cheeks.

'A young woman, but quite emaciated,' his uncle replied. 'She has long black hair, and is dressed in rags. She has a wedding ring on, though. Come along, now.'

'I wish to take a look at her,' Godfrey stated. 'I think I saw such a woman yesterday. You carry on. I shall catch up with you in a minute.'

Godfrey entered the cottage, as Mr. Kimble went on. He took just one look at his dead wife's face. Then he turned to see Silas Marner seated at the hearth, lulling the child. The girl was awake, soothed by warmth and sweet porridge. Her blue eyes looked at Godfrey and the father experienced a mixture of regret and happiness. Then those blue eyes looked away and stared at the weaver's strange face as one hand pulled at Silas's withered cheek. 'You shall take the child tomorrow to the parish?' Godfrey asked as indifferently as he could.

'Who says so?' Silas replied sharply. 'Will they make me do so?'

'An old bachelor like you wouldn't want to keep her, would you?'

'I shall, unless anyone shows me the right to take her away from me,' Silas replied. 'The mother is dead and I guess she has no father. Both of us are alone. My money's gone, I don't know where, and this thing has come from I don't know where. I'm partly amazed.'

'Poor child!' Godfrey exclaimed. 'Let me give something for her clothes.'

He found half-a-guinea in his pocket and thrust it into Silas's hand. Then he rushed and caught up with Mr. Kimble. 'It's not the same woman I saw,' he said. 'The child is pretty and the old weaver wants to keep it. That's strange behaviour from a miser like him. I gave him something to help him. He is not likely to face any opposition from the parish to keep the child.'

'No. It's too late for me to quarrel for the child myself,' Mr. Kimble stated. 'Your aunt is too fat now to overtake the child, if she runs into the fire. She could only sit and grunt like an alarmed sow.'

Godfrey arrived in the white parlour with dry feet and a sense of huge relief. He could

court Nancy without a worry now! There was a chance that Dunsey might spill the beans once he returned, but his silence could be bought. He would ensure, of course, that the child was provided for and taken care of. But while he would never forsake the child, he would never own it either. Maybe the child would be happy not being owned by her father as things stood. It was certain that the father would be happy by not owning the child.

Chapter Ten

Eppie

The fact that Silas Marner was so determined to keep the motherless 'tramp's child' was a matter that was of less surprise and gossip in the village than when he had been robbed. Feelings had softened towards him when his money had been robbed. He had been perceived with suspicion as a crazy loner. He had faced contempt and dislike before because of his miserly, isolated lifestyle. But now there was active sympathy all around for him, especially among the Raveloe women.

Dolly Winthrop's neighbourly quarters were most acceptable to Silas, as Dolly's services came without much preaching or instruction.

But she did suggest one thing to him; to have the child christened.

'I shall ask Mr. Macey to have a word with the parson about it, Master Marner,' Dolly stated to Silas. 'You must think of a name for her when she is christened, though.'

'My mother's name was Hephzibah,' Silas informed her. 'My little sister was named after her.'

'Eh, wasn't it awkward for your little sister to be called by such a difficult name, Master Marner?' Dolly enquired politely.

'Well, we called her Eppie,' Silas replied.

The baby was christened, and the rector arrived at the conclusion that a double baptism was the lesser risk to have in such a case. Silas Marner made himself as clean and tidy as he could, because the occasion demanded it. For the first time in his life, Silas Marner appeared within the Raveloe church, sharing the observances that were regarded sacred by

all his neigbours. He could not equate his old faith with the Raveloe religion. If he could have done it in his earlier life, it would have been only possible thanks to the feelings of kindness and sympathy that had been within him then. But these very feelings had been rendered dormant in him after long years in isolation. Silas had no clear perception about the baptism and the churchgoing. He had only agreed to go with it as Dolly had maintained that it would be good for the child.

As the weeks passed into months, the child only served to create fresh links between the life of the weaver and the lives of others. Unlike the gold that had demanded nothing but worship in isolation, Eppie demanded a lot, seeking and loving the bright sunshine, the songs of birds, living sounds, and living movements. Eppie evoked human kindness in all the eyes that looked at her. The gold had restricted Silas's thoughts in a circle that kept repeating itself. But

Eppie was the circle of life itself. Eppie forced Silas to stretch his thoughts, and look beyond the present into the welcoming future.

The gold had ensured that Silas sat for hours weaving endlessly, with eyes and ears for nothing else but the continuous monotony of his loom, and the repetitive motion of his web. But Eppie had made him break away from his weaving, and made him consider all the breaks as a welcome holiday. Eppie rejuvenated Silas with her freshness, making him glow in the warmth of her joy. Eppie was joy!

Chapter Eleven

Sixteen Years After

Sixteen years passed by. On a bright autumn Sunday, the bells of the Raveloe church were ringing cheerfully to proclaim the end of the morning service. The richer parishioners emerged out of the arched doorway in the tower, greeting each other and talking. They had chosen this bright Sunday morning as perfect for going to church. Among the many members of this well-dressed clan, we shall recognise a few, despite Time having aged them all considerably. The forty something-year-old, tall, blond man doesn't look much different from the twenty-six-year-old Godfrey Cass. He has just put on more

weight, losing only the indescribable youthful look. This loss is perhaps prominent even if the eye is not dull, and the wrinkles are still absent. It is possible that the pretty lady leaning on his arm has experienced more change than her husband. Although not much younger than Godfrey, Nancy's beauty has not faded yet as the years have been kind to her. The mouth is firm yet placid, and the clear, honest glance of the brown eyes seem to denote a nature that has been tested to retain the finest qualities. Even the dress she is wearing is pure and neat, and is more significant than the youthful coquetries.

Mr. and Mrs. Godfrey Cass were the highest titles in Raveloe ever since the old Squire breathed his last. They were now the master and mistress of the Red House. But how can one miss Silas Marner in this gathering? It seems that his large brown eyes have been blessed with a larger vision, just like it is the way with eyes that have been short-sighted in the early years of life, with

the result that they have a less vague but more answering gaze. But with the exception of the eyes, the lapse of sixteen years has taken a toll on the other parts of the weaver's body. Silas's bent shoulders and white hair made him appear much older than the fifty-five years that he had lived. Thankfully, he is accompanied by the fresh blossom of youth, in the form of an eighteen-year-old dimpled girl. She has tried to discipline her curly, auburn hair into smoothness under her brown bonnet, but in vain. Her hair ripples as stubbornly as a brook that flows in the March breeze. The little ringlets refuse to be restrained, breaking away from the comb behind, and revealing themselves below the bonnet-crown.

Eppie cannot but help feeling irritated about her hair as no other girl in Raveloe has hair like she does. Eppie thinks that hair should be smooth instead of curly, and she is very particular even with small things. See how neatly she has folded her prayer-book in her

clean, spotted handkerchief. Silas and Eppie walked up the lonely, sheltered lane on the way home from church. 'O daddy!' Eppie exclaimed, as she kissed Silas energetically. 'I am so happy, my little old daddy!'

'A dear little puss! That's what you are!' Silas exclaimed fondly, and his face reflected great love. 'Now let me carry your prayer-book for you, or else you'll drop it somewhere, the way you are jumping about.'

Eppie was conscious now that her behaviour was under scrutiny, but it was just the observation of a friendly donkey. He was a rather timid donkey, with a log attached to his foot. This particular donkey wished to join in these human trivialities, getting his nose scratched in the process, rather than be disdainfully critical about them. Eppie did not disappoint the donkey, doing the needful as always, although this action came with the burden of the donkey following father and daughter right to their doorstep.

A sharp bark emerged from within, as Eppie put the key in the door. The donkey added to this noise by braying his viewpoint and limped away without further demands. The sharp bark was nothing but a welcome cry from a loving, brown terrier that was awaiting their arrival. It danced at their legs hysterically for a moment, and then scampered inside with a worrying whimper at a tortoise-shell kitten under the loom. Then the terrier ran back with a sharp bark, as if to say, 'I have done my duty as expected to watch over this feeble creature, you see'; while the mother of the kitten lazily sunned her white bosom at the window. She looked at them drowsily, expecting caresses, although it did not appear that she would go out of the way for them.

The presence of animal life was not the only transformation that had taken place in Silas Marner's stone cottage. The living room was conspicuous by the absence of a bed, and the

small interior was now packed with modest furniture, bright and clean enough to approve Dolly Winthrop's eye. The oaken table and the three-cornered oaken chair were hardly something one would expect to see in so poor a cottage. However, this furniture as well as many other things had come from the Red House, under the instructions of Mr. Cass, who had been very kind to the weaver, as everyone in the village stated. For wasn't it the right thing that a man in need should be aided by someone who could well afford to do so? A poor weaver like Marner had reared an orphan child when he had lost all his money, they spoke among themselves. He had no savings now but only that what he made by working hard day by day, and week by week.

The weaving was scarce as Master Marner was not as young anymore. So he spun less and less flax as the days went by. Everyone in Raveloe considered Silas Marner an exceptional man, someone who could not be

matched in the entire village when it came to helping neighbours. The previous perception about him had drastically changed, and Mr. Macey, now a weak old man who was never seen in the village except in his chimney corner or sitting in the sun by his door, thought that when a man like Silas had done something extraordinary like raise an orphan child, it was a heavenly sign that his money would be returned to him. If not that, then the thief would pay for his crime.

A seated Silas watched Eppie with a satisfied look on his face, as she spread and set the clean cloth over the potato pie. It was being warmed up slowly in a safe Sunday fashion. First, it was put in a dry pot over a slowly dying fire, possibly the best substitute for an oven. Silas refused to possess a grate and oven, as he loved his old brown pot just as he loved his old brick hearth. He had found his darling Eppie on that hearth, had he not? The gods of the hearth still

exist for us. Let all new faith be tolerant of this fetishism, lest it bruise its own roots.

Silas had his dinner more silently than he normally did. Soon, he put down his knife and fork to watch absent-mindedly, as Eppie played with Snap and the cat. This activity made Eppie's dinner a lengthy affair. Yet, this pleasant sight was one that stopped wandering thoughts. Eppie, in her dark blue cotton gown, with rippling radiant hair and white rounded chin and throat, laughed merrily as the kitten held on to her shoulder with four claws, resembling a jug-handle design. Snap was perched on Eppie's right hand, and Puss on the other, both of them trying to reach out for a morsel of food, held just out of range by Eppie. Eppie finally caressed both animals, and divided the morsel between them. Eppie decided to stop her play after looking at the clock. 'O daddy, you are wanting to go into the sunshine to smoke your pipe,' she stated. 'But let me clear up first, so

that the house is tidy when godmother arrives. I shall make haste. I won't be long.'

Silas often spoke to Eppie about her past, now that she was older. He had confided in her why he had been a lonely man till she had arrived in his life. It would have been next to impossible for Silas to hide the fact from Eppie that he was not her natural father, after all. Even if one ruled out the tongues that gossiped in Raveloe if Silas had told Eppie he was her natural father, how would he have explained to Eppie who her mother was? So, he had told Eppie the truth long ago, and she was aware that her mother had died in the snow and she had been discovered by Silas on his hearth.

Silas had raised Eppie with a peculiar love that was tender in nature. In their relative isolation from the village, Eppie had been spared the influence of the village talk and habits. So, Eppie was still fresh and childlike, and questions regarding her parentage did

not arise in her mind. In fact, the first time it occurred to Eppie that her mother might have had a husband was when Silas displayed the wedding ring taken from her dead mother's finger. The weaver had carefully preserved the ring in a little shoe-shaped box. He had entrusted this box to Eppie when she had grown up, and she opened it to look at the ring often. But she rarely thought about the father that this ring was supposed to symbolise. Didn't she, Eppie reasoned, have a father who was very close to her heart? Didn't this father love her more than all the fathers in the village loved their daughters? Rather than the thought of her real father, what was pressing on Eppie's mind were questions like who her mother was, and how she died in that loneliness.

Mrs. Winthrop was closest to Eppie after Silas, and her presence made Eppie realise that a mother must be really special indeed. She repeatedly asked Silas to recall the memory as

to how her mother looked and how he had discovered her lying in the snow against the furze bush. 'Father, if I were to marry, should I be married with my mother's ring?' Eppie asked Silas, after a long silence. Silas started, although he had been thinking about the same thing.

'Why, Eppie?' he enquired. 'Have you been a-thinking on it?'

'Only this last week, father,' Eppie replied. 'Ever since Aaron talked to me about it.'

'What did he say?' Silas asked, subdued yet anxious. 'Well, he said he would like to be married as he was about to be twenty-four, and had a lot of gardening work now that Mr. Mott's given up. He is visiting Mr. Cass's regular twice a week now, and once to Mr. Osgood's. He told me that they are going to take him on at the Rectory soon.'

'Who is it that he wants to marry?' Silas enquired. 'Why, me, daddy,' Eppie laughed, with prominent dimples, as she kissed her

father's cheek. 'As if he'd want to marry someone else.'

'You wish to marry him, do you, dear?' Silas asked.

'Sometime, yes,' Eppie replied. 'But I don't know when. Everybody gets married sometime, Aaron says. But I told him that this wasn't true. Look at father, I said. He's never been married.'

'That's true,' Silas stated. 'Your father was a lone man till you arrived in his life.'

'But you'll never be alone again, father,' Eppie said lovingly. 'Aaron said he could never think of taking me away from you. He wants us to all live together, so you don't need to work anymore. He said he'll be as good as a son to you.'

'Would you like that, Eppie?' Silas asked.

'I wouldn't mind it, father,' Eppie stated simply. 'I wouldn't want you to work as much as you do. But if not for that, I'd rather that things be just the way they are. I'm very happy, father. I like that Aaron is so fond of me, and

that he comes to visit us often. I want him to behave nicely with you. He does behave nicely with you, doesn't he, father?'

'Yes, my child,' Silas replied. 'No one could behave any better. He is his mother's child, after all.'

'But I do not want any change to happen,' Eppie declared. 'I want things to go on and on, just the way they are. But Aaron wants a change, and he did make me cry a bit, just a bit, when he said that I didn't care for him. He said that if I cared for him, I would want us to be married like he does.'

'Ah, my blessed child,' Silas said, putting down his pipe as it was futile to pretend to smoke any longer. 'We shall ask Aaron's mother, Mrs. Winthrop, what she thinks about it. She'll know if that is the right thing to do. But one has to think about this, Eppie. Things will change, no matter if we like it or not. Things won't go on the same way, just as they are. I

shall grow older and more helpless, a burden to you. I don't wish to say you'd ever think of me as a burden, of course. But it would make things hard for you. I'd like to think that you have someone else behind you, someone young and strong to take care of you all your life, when I'm gone,' Silas said reflectively, staring at the ground as he finished. 'So, would you like me to be married, father?' Eppie asked with a tremble in her voice. 'I shall never say no, Eppie,' Silas stated emphatically. 'But we have to ask your godmother. She'll know what's right for you, and her son as well.'

'There they come, father,' Eppie exclaimed suddenly. 'Let us go and meet them. Oh, the pipe!' Eppie said, lifting the medicinal appliance from the ground. 'Don't you want it lit again, father?'

'Nay, child,' Silas replied. 'I've had enough for one day. I think a little of it does me more good than too much at once.'

Chapter Twelve

A Childless Couple

When Silas and Eppie were talking, Miss Priscilla Lammeter was countering her sister's proposal that it was a better idea to take tea at the Red House, permitting her father to have a long nap rather than driving home to the Warrens, right after dinner. The family of four were seated around the parlour table with the Sunday dessert laid out before them. It consisted of fresh filberts, apples and pears that were ornamented with leaves by Nancy, before the church bells had rung.

A great transformation had been witnessed in that dark parlour ever since the wifeless

reign of the old squire, when Godfrey had been a bachelor. Nancy had removed all signs of sporting and outdoor activity from the parlour to another room. These involved the guns, whips and the walking sticks as well. Nancy had brought about an ambience of tranquility and love into the Red House and the parlour no longer looked dreary.

'Now, father,' Nancy stated. 'Must you go home to tea? Mayn't you just stay with us? It's likely to be a beautiful evening.'

'My dear, you must ask Priscilla,' replied the old man, who had been talking to Godfrey about the increased rate of the poor and hard times. 'You see, she manages me and the farm as well.'

'It is good that I do that, father,' Priscilla replied. 'You might give yourself death with rheumatism, otherwise. As for the farm, if anything turns out wrong, as is expected in these hard times, there is nothing that kills a man more than having nobody to find fault with, but himself. The best way to be master these days is to have someone else give the orders so that one can keep the blaming in your own hands. I think it would save many a man the bother of a stroke.'

'Well, my dear,' her father laughed. 'I never said you don't manage the farm for the good of everyone.'

'Then manage, so that you may stay for tea, Priscilla,' Nancy declared, as she patted her sister's arm. 'Come, let us walk around the garden while father has his nap.'

'My dear sister, he shall have a wonderful nap in the gig, as I shall drive,' Priscilla replied. 'I can't stay for tea, I'm afraid. But let us take a walk around the garden while the horse is being readied.'

As the sisters walked, Priscilla stated it was good that Godfrey was making an exchange of land with cousin Osgood. 'It is good that your husband is beginning with dairying,' she said, pressing her sister's hand lovingly. 'It will be good to fill your mind. You'll never feel sad when you've got a dairy.'

'But it won't make up to Godfrey, dear Priscilla,' Nancy replied sadly. 'A dairy is not much to a man. I am low only when I think of what he wants. I'm happy with whatever we are blessed with. If only I could make him happy!'

'It makes me impatient the way men always keep wanting,' Priscilla exclaimed haughtily. 'They are never satisfied with what they have, and they can't be comfortably seated in their chairs, even if they do not have aches or pains. They must have a pipe sticking out of their mouths to make them more comfortable or else they must be swallowing something strong. Thankfully though, our father was not such kind of a man. If only God had chosen to make you ugly like me, Nancy, the men wouldn't have chased you so hard, and we might have kept

to our own family. That way, we wouldn't have to associate with folks that have uneasy blood running in their veins.'

'Oh, please don't say that, Priscilla,' Nancy exclaimed, guilty that she had brought about this outburst from her sister. 'Godfrey doesn't give anyone any occasion to find fault with him. It is but natural that he be disappointed at not having any children. All men like having someone to work for and save money for. I know many men who would hanker more than he does at not having any children. Godfrey is the best husband I could have ever asked for.'

'Yes, I know,' Priscilla stated, smiling sarcastically. 'I know the way wives set up someone to abuse their husbands, and then turn around to defend their husbands, praising them as if they were up for sale. But we must go back now as father will be awaiting me.'

One painful thread of Nancy's married life was revived after the conversation with Priscilla

in the garden, lingering on in her memory even after her sister's departure. Now, Nancy reflected if she had done everything in her power to keep her husband happy. Had she been right in resisting when Godfrey had wanted to adopt a child? The suggestion of adoption by Godfrey had caused much pain to Nancy, simply because the concept of adopting a child was very remote in those days. Nancy had an opinion on it just as she had a strong opinion on everything else. Nancy acted resolutely on these opinions that became her principles in life. These became a code that were rooted firmly in her mind, and grew there like grass. For example, a young Nancy insisted dressing like Priscilla simply because it was considered that sisters should dress alike. If she wanted to wear a gown dyed with cheese colouring, Nancy would wear that, no matter what people said or thought about it.

Nancy's view regarding adoption was just this: To adopt a child just because you had

been denied children of your own was an act of defying Providence. Nancy was firm in her rigid belief that if you chose your child, the adopted child would never turn out well. As the child was not related by blood, it would be more of a curse than a blessing. This peculiar way of thinking followed by Nancy applied in other cases as well. She would have abandoned making a purchase at a certain place if an obstacle had presented itself to stop her three times successively in the form of rain, or any other heavenly sending. She saw these signs as a heavenly warning, and feared a calamity like a broken limb or a deeper misfortune, if one persisted despite these warning signs. So, while Godfrey had tried his best to argue that they adopt the weaver's daughter, Nancy had not agreed.

But even Godfrey had not realised that Silas would rather part with his life than with Eppie. He had assumed that the weaver would gladly

part with his daughter, should she encounter good fortune. 'Many men would have been angry with me for opposing their wishes,' Nancy thought to herself. 'But Godfrey, although hurt, has never been angry with me for refusing to adopt the weaver's daughter. Other men might have abandoned me thinking that I have brought ill-luck to the marriage by being motherless. Maybe, he could have been happier if he had married a woman who would have given birth to children. But then, she would have irritated him by other ways.'

The last assumption was also a source of comfort for Nancy, and she concluded that no other wife could give Godfrey so much tenderness. She had irritated him just once with that single act of denial, when he had insisted on adoption. Godfrey, on the other hand, found it impossible to tell Nancy about his past, as he was sure that Nancy would be so repulsed about Eppie as to never recover from the shock.

So he decided to keep this secret lodged deep in his heart, suffering instead. As a man or a woman reaches middle age, they mostly realise that life cannot be thoroughly joyous when the hearth is conspicuous by the absence of children. Godfrey's heart experienced a void like that on his hearth, and he was envious of the fathers who were greeted by excited young voices upon their return home. Furthermore, Godfrey's conscience always troubled him about Eppie, and Nancy's refusal to adopt her, made his heart even heavier.

But it was tea-time, and Godfrey had not returned home yet. The servant Jane added to Nancy's worries by saying that she had seen people rushing together somewhere, and that she hoped nothing had happened. Nancy worried more and more, wishing Godfrey would come home soon.

Chapter Thirteen

The Truth is Revealed

The door opened at the other end of the room, and Nancy felt it was Godfrey. She turned from the window and approached him.

'Dear, I'm so glad you've come. I was getting...'

Nancy paused all of a sudden, as Godfrey lay down his hat with a trembling hand. Then, he turned towards her with a shrunken face and a strange look as if he'd seen a ghost. She laid a hand on his arm, not daring to speak again, but he did not return the touch. Godfrey flung himself onto his chair instead. He spoke clearly after the door was closed.

'I returned as soon as I could, to stop anyone from telling you, but me,' Godfrey said, after asking Nancy to sit on a chair opposite him. 'I've had a great shock, but I care more about the shock you'll receive.'

'Is it father and Priscilla?' Nancy exclaimed with a quivering lip, clasping her hands tightly together on her lap.

'No, it's no one that's alive,' Godfrey stated. 'It's my brother Dunstan. We lost sight of him sixteen years ago. We've just found him, rather, just found his body- his skeleton.'

Nancy felt a deep sense of relief as the look of horror on Godfrey's face had alarmed her. She waited in comparative calm to hear what else he had to say.

'The Stone-pit has gone dry all of a sudden,' Godfrey continued. 'I suppose this is on account of the draining. There he lies! In fact, Dunstan has lain there for sixteen long years, wedged between two great stones. We've found his

watch and seals, and my gold-handled hunting-whip, with my name on it. He took it away without my knowledge, the day he went to sell Wildfire. That was the last time he was seen.'

Godfrey paused, as it was not easy for him to say what he was about to say to Nancy next.

'What do you think happened?' a surprised Nancy asked. 'Did he drown himself?'

The surprise Nancy felt was largely on account of Godfrey's deep reaction to what had happened many years ago to an unloved brother, of whom worse things had been expected.

'No,' Godfrey replied in a low voice, 'He fell in. Dunstan was the thief! It was he who had robbed Silas Marner!'

The blood rushed to Nancy's face at this statement. She felt both shock and shame, as she had been raised to consider even the slightest association with crime as a dishonour.

'Oh Godfrey!' she exclaimed in pity and compassion, feeling that her husband might

feel dishonour even more than her.

'The money was there in the pit,' Godfrey continued. 'All of Silas Marner's money. It's been collected, and they are taking the skeleton to the Rainbow. But I came back as you must know the facts as they are.'

Godfrey was silent after that and stared at the ground for a full two minutes. Nancy restrained herself from saying a few comforting words as she sensed instinctively that something more was coming. Godfrey lifted his eyes slowly and looked at Nancy.

'Everything comes into the open sooner or later, Nancy,' he stated. 'Our secrets are discovered when the Almighty God wills it. I've lived with a secret lodged in my heart, like a dagger. But I shan't keep it from you any longer. I will not have you know it from someone else, and neither will I have you know it after my death. I shall tell you right now! It's been 'I will' and 'I won't' all my life. But not anymore. I am

sure of myself now.'

Nancy's dread had resurfaced and husband's and wife's eyes were awestruck when they met each other, as in a crisis where love is suspended.

'Nancy, I hid something from you when I married you,' Godfrey continued slowly. 'I should have told you that. The woman that Marner discovered dead in the snow, that wretched woman, was none other than my wife. Eppie is my child!'

Godfrey paused now, unsure about the consequences of his confession, and dreading it. Nancy sat still as a statue, but her eyes dropped and refused to meet her husband's eyes. She appeared pale and her hands clasped each other on her lap.

'I know you'll never think the same of me again,' Godfrey stated, his voice shaking slightly. Nancy was silent.

'I shouldn't have kept the matter a secret from you. I shouldn't have left the child

unowned,' Godfrey ranted. 'But I couldn't bear the thought of having to give you up, Nancy. I was led astray into marrying her and I suffered terribly for it.'

Nancy was still silent, with her eyes cast downwards. Godfrey expected that she would get up soon and tell him that she was leaving for her father's. There was no blaming her for this decision, as with her simple, severe notions, this was a black crime! But when Nancy spoke, there was no anger in her voice. There was only deep regret.

'Godfrey, if you had told me this sixteen years ago, we could have done our duty towards the child,' she stated. 'Do you think I would have refused to take her in my home if I'd known she was yours?'

That was the moment when Godfrey felt the bitterness of his error that had not only been proven futile, but had also defeated its own end. He had not fully gauged this wife with whom

he had lived with for so many years.

'Oh, Godfrey,' Nancy spoke agitatedly, 'If only we'd had her from the very first, and you'd taken her in, as you ought to have, she would have loved me for her mother. You'd also have been happier with me. Our life would be just like we had wanted it to be.'

Nancy stopped talking as her tears fell incessantly.

'But if I had told you, you wouldn't have married me then, Nancy,' Godfrey protested, in order to prove that his decision had not been sheer folly. 'You might think you would have now, Nancy. But you wouldn't then. With your father's pride, and your pride, you'd have hated to have anything to do with me after the gossip and the scandal.'

'I can't say about that, Godfrey,' Nancy said. 'But I can tell you this! I would have never married anybody else. Nothing is as good as it seems beforehand. Even our marriage wasn't,'

she smiled sadly.

'I'm a worse man than you had ever thought, Nancy,' Godfrey said sadly. 'Can you ever forgive me?'

'You've made up the wrong done to me, Godfrey,' Nancy replied. 'You've been good to me for fifteen years. You did wrong to someone else, and I doubt if you can ever repair that wrong.'

'But we can take in Eppie now,' Godfrey stated. 'I don't care if the world knows about it. I shall be open and honest for the rest of my life.'

'She's grown up now. It'll be difficult coming to us now,' Nancy replied, shaking her head sadly. 'But your duty demands that you acknowledge her and provide for her. I'll do my part and pray to God that she loves me as well.'

'Then let us go to Silas Marner's house tonight itself,' Godfrey urged. 'We shall leave when everything is quiet at the Stone-pits.'

Chapter Fourteen

A Father's Love

That night, between eight and nine, Eppie and Silas were seated together, alone in the cottage. The events of the afternoon had caused great excitement to Silas and he had requested Mrs. Winthrop and Aaron, who had stayed back after everyone had left, to leave them alone. This excitement did not fade away, but only grew stronger, making sleep a distinct impossibility. Eppie held her father's hands and looked at him. The recovered gold lay on the table before them, illuminated by candlelight. The very gold that used to be Silas's only joy once upon a time! It was back again!

Silas had confided in Eppie how he used to count the gold each night and how lonely he had been without it, till she had appeared in his life.

'I first thought that you might change into the gold again,' he said to her. 'I thought I'd be happy to have the gold back. But then, had it returned it would have been a curse, driving you away from me. Oh, Eppie, you have no idea what your old father Silas felt for you.'

'I know now, father,' Eppie stated. 'If it were not for you, I'd have been taken to the workhouse, where there would be nobody to love me.'

'The blessing was mine, my precious child,' Silas insisted. 'If you hadn't been sent to save me, I would have gone to my grave in my misery. The money had been taken from me, and kept safely till you needed it. Oh, it's wonderful! Our life's wonderful.'

Silas sat silently for a while before stating, 'The gold has no hold over me now. I wonder

if it ever could again. I doubt it would if I lost you, Eppie.'

A knock on the door interrupted their conversation and Eppie was forced to answer the door, without replying to Silas. She looked beautiful with tears flowing down her eyes and a slight flush on her cheeks. On opening the door, when she spotted Mr. and Mrs. Godfrey Cass, the flush deepened. She opened the door wide after a little rustic curtsy, and the two entered.

'We're disturbing you very late, my dear,' Mrs. Cass said, taking Eppie's hand and staring at her with interest and admiration. Nancy was nervous and pale. Eppie placed chairs for Mr. and Mrs. Cass, and stood against Silas opposite them.

'Well, Marner,' Godfrey began firmly. 'It is indeed comforting for me to see you with your money again, as you've been deprived of it for many years. One of my family did this wrong to you and this fact causes me further grief. I

feel bound to make up for this in every way. Whatever I can do for you will be nothing but paying a debt. But there are other things I'm beholden to you for as well.'

Godfrey paused as it had been decided between him and Nancy that the subject of his fatherhood should be raised rather carefully. If possible, the disclosure should be put off for later, and revealed to Eppie gradually. Nancy had suggested this, as it would ease Eppie's pain in perceiving the strained relations between her mother and father. Silas, who was always ill at ease when his 'betters' like Mr. Cass addressed him, replied with some constraint, 'Sir, I have a lot to thank you for already. As for the robbery, I don't think of it as a loss. Even if I did, you are not answerable for it.'

'You might think of it as that, Marner,' Godfrey replied. 'But I can never do the same. I hope you will let me act in a way that I feel is just. I know you are a contented man as you've worked hard all your life.'

'Yes, sir,' Silas replied. 'My work is what I held on to, when everything else was taken away from me.'

'This country has given you good trade, as a lot of linen-weaving was demanded. But you're getting old now, Marner. It's time for you to rest. You look rather weighed down, although you aren't very old. Are you, Marner?'

'Fifty-five, sir,' Silas replied.

'Oh, you'll live at least thirty years more. That money on the table is not a great amount. It won't last that long, even if you put it out to interest or make it last till your end. You've also had to provide for two for many years now.'

'I'm in fear of no want, sir,' Silas replied, unsure of what Godfrey was getting at. 'We shall do very well, Eppie and me. Few working folks have got so much saved. I know it's not much to you gentlefolks. But I think it's a lot for me. We want little, after all.'

'Just the garden, father,' Eppie declared, blushing immediately as she uttered these words.

'You love a garden, do you my dear?' Nancy stated, thinking that this new information could help her husband in his quest. 'We have something in common then, as I devote a lot of time to the garden.'

'Yes, there's plenty of gardening to be done at the Red House,' Godfrey backed up his wife, surprised at the ease this proposition offered as a logical solution to a difficult approach. 'You've done so much for Eppie for sixteen years, Marner. Wouldn't it be a great comfort for you if she is well provided for in life? She looks blooming and in fine health, but not someone who is cut out to face hardships in life. She doesn't look like a girl of working parents. You would like to see that Eppie is taken care of by someone who can leave her well off, and make a fine lady of her.'

A momentary flush appeared on Silas's face, and disappeared like a passing glow. Eppie wondered how Mr. Cass could speak about so many things that had no connection with reality. But his words had made Silas both uncomfortable and hurt.

'I didn't get your meaning, sir,' he replied, not in possession of words to express his feelings about Mr. Cass's statement.

'Well, what I mean to say is this, Marner,' Godfrey stated, anxious to come to the point quickly, 'You know Mrs. Cass and I have no children. There is no heir to benefit by whatever we own, which is more than enough for the two of us. We would like someone in the place of a daughter to us. We would like to have Eppie, and treat her just like our own child. I think it would be greatly comforting for you to see her settled in your old age. After all, you've taken so much pains to raise her so well. You are deserving of every reward for that. I'm

sure that Eppie will always love you, and be indebted to you. She would come and see you very often, and we shall do everything to make you comfortable.'

A man like Godfrey Cass, speaking when embarrassed, is bound to blunder on words that are rougher than his intentions. Eppie had quietly passed her arm behind Silas's head, and rested it there caressingly. She felt him trembling violently. The weaver was silent for a while after Mr. Cass finished speaking; powerless under the onslaught of conflicting, painful emotions. Eppie's heart burst with the thought that her father faced so much suffering, and she was just about to bend down and talk to him, when Silas spoke faintly,

'Speak, my child, Eppie,' he said. 'I won't stand in your way.'

Eppie stepped forward without shyness this time, as the thought that her father was suffering had removed that kind of self-consciousness.

She curtsied Mrs. Cass and Mr. Cass and said, 'Thank you, ma'am. Thank you, sir. But I cannot leave my father, nor own anybody except him. I do not wish to be a lady. I cannot give up the folks I have been used to. Thank you all the same.'

With trembling lips, Eppie returned by her father's side, and held him round the neck. Silas grasped her hand with a subdued sob. There were tears in Nancy's eyes, but whatever sympathy she felt for Eppie was divided naturally with sadness because of her husband. She did not dare to speak, wondering what he might be thinking.

Godfrey felt an irritation, similar to the feelings all of us experience when we face an unexpected hurdle. He had been full of penance, and resolved to rectify the error made by him in the limited time he had at his disposal. But he was thoroughly unprepared at the opposition to his predetermined plan that he thought to

be perfect. His irritation turned to anger now.

'Let me tell you that I've got a claim on you, Eppie,' he declared. 'It is the strongest of all claims. Marner, it is my duty to own Eppie as my child, and provide for her. For Eppie is my own child! Her mother was my wife! I have a natural claim on her that no other claim can stand against.'

Eppie started violently and became white as stone. Silas on the other hand, felt differently. He had dreaded earlier that Eppie's mind might not be co-related with his and experienced a sense of relief at Eppie's reply. Now the spirit of resistance in him was unleashed, and it was full of the fierce protectiveness of a parent.

'Then, sir,' he replied almost bitterly. 'Why didn't you say so sixteen years ago? Why didn't you step forward to claim her before I did so, and begin to love her? Why have you come to my home to take her away now, when it's better to take away the heart from my body instead?

God bestowed her to me only because you turned your back upon her. He sees Eppie as mine, and you, sir, have no right to her.'

This was the Silas of old, and this accent of bitterness had resurfaced again from his dreaded, youthful days.

'I was wrong, Marner,' Godfrey replied, feeling the full edge of the weaver's words. 'I know that! I have repented my actions since.'

'I'm happy to hear that, sir,' Marner said, with increasing excitement. 'But repenting does not change what's been going on for sixteen years. You coming here now, and declaring that you are her father, does not change a thing between us. It does not alter the feelings inside us. She's been calling me her father ever since she could pronounce the word.'

'You might choose to look at this matter a little differently, Marner,' Godfrey stated, awed at the unexpected manner in which the weaver logically put forth his arguments. 'It's not that she is being taken away from you, and that you'll never set eyes on her again. She'll be near you, and see you often. She'll feel just the same towards you.'

'Just the same?' Silas exclaimed bitterly. 'How will she feel just the same when we eat the same food, and drink of the same cup! Just the same? That's idle talk! You'd cut us into two!'

Godfrey, inexperienced to gauge the weaver's simple words, was angry again. He felt the weaver was being rather selfish to oppose Eppie's welfare for his own vested interests. This was a normal thought process for people whose power of sacrifice has never been tested in life.

'I would have thought, Marner, that your love for Eppie would make you rejoice in her well-being,' he said severely. 'Your own life is uncertain, and she might marry some low working man as a result. I couldn't make her well-off, no matter how hard I tried then. I'm sorry to hurt you after all that you've done for Eppie, but I feel I must do my duty for my daughter, as a father should.'

It was difficult to judge if Silas was more affected by this speech or Eppie. Eppie though, was busy in her thoughts as she listened to this war of words between her old, long-loved father, and this new, unfamiliar father, who had suddenly arrived to form the missing piece in that jigsaw puzzle. That black shadow without features that had placed the ring around her mother's finger once upon a time! The implications of this fatherhood were made definite to Eppie by Godfrey's last speech. Not that they influenced or changed Eppie's earlier decision in any way. In fact, Eppie was repulsed by this new father, and the promises that he made.

On the other hand, Silas was alarmed at the prospect of losing Eppie. 'Speak to the child,' he said, with great difficulty. 'I shall not hinder anything.'

Even Nancy, sensible though she was, shared her husband's view that Marner was not being reasonable in his wish to retain the child, after her real father had asserted his right. She did feel that it was tough on the weaver, but the righteous code that she had abided by all her life demanded that a father by blood held a claim over his child, more than anyone else. So, Nancy was relieved when she heard Silas's last words, as she believed that their wish was fulfilled.

'Eppie, my dear,' Godfrey addressed his daughter with a little embarrassment now, as he was aware that Eppie was old enough to judge him. 'We shall always want you to show love and gratitude to someone who's acted as your father for so many years, and we shall endeavour that you can make him comfortable in every manner possible. But we do hope and wish that you'll come to love us too. I know that I haven't been the father I should have been all these years. But now I wish to do all that is in my power to be a good and loving father for the rest of my life, and take care of you as my only child. You'll have the best mother in my wife as it's a blessing you have never known.'

'I shall treasure you, my dear,' Nancy said gently. 'Our life shall be complete when we have our daughter.'

Eppie did not step forward and curtsy this time. Instead, she held Silas's hand firmly.

'Thank you for your offers, ma'am and sir,' Eppie spoke coldly this time. 'Your offers are great, and beyond my wishes. But I should have no joy in life if I were separated from my father. We've known happiness together and I can't think of happiness without him. He has taken care of me from the first, and I shall love him till the end. No one shall ever come between him and me.'

'But you must be sure, Eppie,' Silas said gently. 'You must ensure you will never be sorry, as you have made your choice to stay with poor folks when you could have the best of the best.'

'I can never be sorry, father,' Eppie declared. 'I have no idea what to do with fine things as I am not used to them. Why should I care for them?'

Nancy gave Godfrey a pained, questioning glance. But he had his eyes on the floor and he was thinking deeply.

'What you say is but natural, my dear,' Nancy decided to do the talking. 'You should stick to those who brought you up. But you also owe a duty to your natural father. I think you should walk into your father's home if he opens it for you.'

'I have only one father,' Eppie declared proudly, as tears gathered in her eyes. 'This is my home, and I can't think of any other. I wasn't raised to be a lady, and I like the working folks. I've also promised to marry a working man who will live with my father and help me take care of him.'

Godfrey stared at Nancy with a flushed face and teary eyes. He seemed frustrated and defeated. 'Let us leave!' He said in an undertone.

'We shall not talk about this any longer now,' Nancy said to Eppie as she rose from her seat. 'But my dear, we are your well-wishers, and yours as well, Marner. We shall visit you again. It is late now.'

Nancy covered her husband's sudden departure in this manner, as Godfrey had headed straight for the door, incapable of uttering another word.

Chapter Fifteen

Eppie Takes a Decision

Nancy and Godfrey walked home silently. Godfrey flung himself on a chair while Nancy stood beside her husband, not wanting to leave him alone. Their eyes met after a while, and it was the silent mutual gaze of a trusting husband and wife. There was no movement, and it was like the first moment of refuge after a great calamity. It was not to be interrupted with either speech or action that would distract the senses from the joys of rest.

Godfrey extended his hand, and as Nancy put hers in it, he drew her towards him. 'That's ended!' He said, and they kissed.

'I'm afraid we must abandon the hope of having her as a daughter,' Nancy stated. 'It won't be right to do so against her will.'

'No!' Godfrey agreed decisively. 'It's too late now. Marner was right. I won't let anyone know that she's my daughter, but I think I shall put it in my will. I think its Aaron Winthrop she's engaged to. I saw them together at church.'

'Well, he's sober and industrious,' Nancy said, trying to make it cheerful.

'She's a very pretty girl, isn't she, Nancy?'

'Yes, dear. She has your hair and eyes.'

'I think she hated the fact that I was her father.'

'I think she couldn't bear the thought of Marner not being her father,' Nancy stated.

'She thinks I did wrong to her mother,' Godfrey said. 'She thinks me worse than I am. But that cannot be helped, as she can never know the truth. It's part of my punishment for my daughter to hate me. I shouldn't have acted

like the fool I have. Nothing but evil could have come from that marriage. I shirked my duty as a father too. But I still got you Nancy, and yet I grumble about not having anything else. I'm not deserving.'

'You've been good to me, Godfrey,' Nancy replied. 'My troubles would disappear if you are happy with what we have.'

'Well, it's never too late to mend things there,' Godfrey stated. 'Even though it's too late to mend some things.'

Chapter Sixteen

The End or the Beginning?

'Eppie, there's something I've been wanting to do,' Silas said to Eppie over breakfast the next morning.

'Now that the money is back, we can do it. We'll leave the house in your godmother's care and set out tomorrow.'

'Where to, daddy?' A surprised Eppie asked.

'To the town I was born,' Silas replied. 'I wish to see Mr. Paston, the minister. Something might have come up to reveal that I was innocent of the robbery. I also want to talk to him about the religion of this countryside.'

Eppie was very happy, as there was a chance to see a strange country which was wonderful. She could return and tell Aaron all about it. Silas and Eppie travelled together to reach Lantern Yard, but the weaver was in for a huge shock. Lantern Yard had disappeared, replaced by a large factory. Silas could not find his old friends, including the minister, Mr. Paston. Silas and Eppie returned sadly to Raveloe.

Soon, Raveloe was experiencing that time of the year when weddings were in fashion. This was the season when the old-fashioned gardens were blooming with great lilacs and laburnums. Even the sunshine was warmer than usual on the lilac tufts the morning Eppie got married. She walked across the churchyard, and down the village in a light dress, giving the appearance of being attired in pure white. Mrs. Godfrey Cass had pleaded with Eppie that she be allowed to provide her wedding dress, and had asked Eppie to choose it. Eppie's hair resembled the dash of gold on a lily. She held her husband's arm with one hand and the hand of her father with the other. 'You won't be giving me away, father,' she had said to Silas before they left for church. 'You'll be receiving Aaron as a son.'

Dolly Winthrop walked behind her husband, and thus ended the small bridal procession. Plenty of eyes were there to witness this lovely sight. Priscilla Lammeter was happy that she and her father had arrived to witness it. They had come to keep Nancy company as Mr. Godfrey Cass had to leave for Lytherley, for special reasons. It was a pity as he had ordered a grand wedding feast at the Rainbow that he wouldn't be able to attend himself.

The procession passed the Red House, and reached the humbler part of the village called Raveloe. They greeted Mr. Macey at his door as he was too affected by rheumatism to walk. After all, he was the one who had predicted that

Marner would get his money back. The guests gathered at the Rainbow an hour before the appointed hour of the feast. They talked at leisure about the strange history of the weaver and how he had obtained a blessing from God by raising a motherless child. They raised a hearty cheer as the bridal group finally approached the yard of the Rainbow.

Ben Winthrop decided to join the crowd gathered there, accept their congratulations, and regale them with his popular jokes, instead of accompanying the bridal party to the Stone-Pits. They would join the feast after their visit there, while he would stay on here. Eppie had a large garden at the Stone-Pits now, where alterations had been considerably made, all thanks to the kind Mr. Cass so that Silas Marner's large family would be benefitted. This was because Silas and Eppie had declared that they preferred staying at the Stone-Pits, rather than settling into any new home. Eppie's new garden at the

Stone-Pits was fenced with stones on either side, but an open fence stood right in front of it. The flowers shone through this open fence with great happiness as the four united people approached them now. 'Oh, father!' Eppie said in joy. 'What a pretty home we have! I think no one could be happier than we are!'

About the Author

■ George Elliot

George Elliot (22 November 1819- 22 December 1880) was the pen name of Mary Ann Evans, an English novelist who was one of the leading writers of the Victorian era. She has authored seven novels, including The Mill on the Floss, Middlemarch and Silas Marner. Most of her stories are set in provincial England and are popular for their realism and psychological insight.

She used a male pen name so that her works were taken seriously. Those days, female authors were stereotyped as writers of lighthearted romances, a myth Elliot wanted to break, and shattered successfully. Middlemarch has been described by some as the greatest novel in the English language. Silas Marner is a simple tale of love and hope, but also deals with issues like religion, community and industrialisation.

■ List of Main Characters

Silas Marner - He is a simple, honest, and kindhearted weaver. Silas arrives in Raveloe after losing his faith and lives for fifteen years as a solitary miser. After his money is stolen, his faith and trust are restored by his adopted daughter, Eppie.

Godfrey Cass - Godfrey is the eldest son of Squire Cass. He is good-natured but selfish and weak-hearted. He refuses to acknowledge his child Eppie and pursues his selfish interests. Later wants to adopt Eppie when he is childless.

Eppie – She is adopted by Silas Marner after her mother dies. She is the biological child of Godfrey Cass and Molly Farren. Eppie is pretty and spirited and loves Silas unquestioningly, choosing him over her natural father.

Nancy Lammeter– She is Godfrey's devoted wife. Nancy is pretty, caring, and stubborn, and lives her life by a strict code of rules.

Dunstan Cass - Godfrey's younger brother who is cruel, lazy, and unscrupulous, and loves gambling and drinking. He also steals Silas Marner's gold.

Squire Cass - The Squire is lazy, self-satisfied, and short-tempered. But he is also the richest man in Raveloe.

Dolly Winthrop - She is the wheelwright's wife. Dolly later becomes Eppie's godmother and mother-in-law. She is kind, patient, and devout.

Molly Farren – She is Godfrey's secret wife and Eppie's mother. Molly has been destroyed by her addiction to opium and alcohol.

William Dane - Silas's best friend in Lantern Yard, William Dane frames Silas for theft to marry his fiancée, Sarah.

■ Questions

Chapter 1

- *Who was Silas Marner?*
- *Why was Marner accused of stealing? Who accused him and*
- *how?*

Chapter 2

- *Describe the weaver's daily routine in Raveloe.*
- *What made Silas Marner turn into a miser?*

Chapter 3

- *Who was Godfrey? How did Dunstan blackmail him?*
- *What was Godfrey's dark secret? What did Godfrey sacrifice to save himself?*

Chapter 4

- *Describe what happened after Dunsey took Wildfire to sell it.*
- *How and why did Dunsey steal the weaver's gold? Describe.*

Chapter 5

- *Where was Marner when Dunsey arrived at his cottage? Why did Marner leave the door unlocked?*
- *Whom did Marner suspect of stealing? Why?*

Chapter 6

- *What was the evidence discovered after the robbery?*
- *What decision did Godfrey take before he went to sleep at night? Why?*

Chapter 7

- *What was Silas Marner's reaction when his gold was stolen?*
- *Why was Godfrey so sad on Christmas Eve?*

Chapter 8

- *Who was Molly Farren? Why did she travel to Raveloe with her child?*
- *How did the child end up in Marner's cottage? Describe in detail.*

Chapter 9

- *Why was Godfrey shocked to see Silas Marner with the child?*
- *Why did Godfrey go to fetch Dolly?*

Chapter 10

- *Who was Eppie?*
- *How did Eppie's arrival change Silas Marner's life?*

Chapter 11

- *Describe the change in the appearances of Godfrey, Marner and Eppie after sixteen years.*
- *Who had proposed marriage to Eppie? What was Marner's reaction?*

Chapter 12

- *How did Nancy change the interiors of the Red House? Describe.*
- *Describe the conversation between Nancy and Priscilla in the garden.*

Chapter 13

- *How did Silas Marner get his gold back? Describe.*
- *What secret did Godfrey reveal to his wife? What was Nancy's reaction?*

Chapter 14

- *Why did Godfrey and Nancy visit Marner's house?*
- *Why did Marner refuse to hand Eppie over to Godfrey?*

Chapter 15

- *What was Eppie's decision? Do you think it was the right one?*
- *What were the reactions of Marner, Godfrey and Nancy at Eppie's decision?*

Chapter 16

- *Briefly describe Eppie's wedding in your own words.*
- *Why do you think Godfrey was not present at Eppie's wedding? Explain in detail.*